The Nutcracker

Contributing writer
Carolyn Quattrocki

Cover illustration   Illustrations
Linda Graves Susan Spellman

Louis Weber, C.E.O.
Publications International, Ltd.
7373 North Cicero Avenue
Lincolnwood, Illinois 60646

Manufactured in U.S.A.

8 7 6 5 4 3 2 1

ISBN: 0-7853-1362-1

PUBLICATIONS INTERNATIONAL, LTD.
Candy Cane Books is a trademark of Publications International, Ltd.

One Christmas Eve in Germany, a long time ago, Marie and her brother Fritz were opening some of their gifts. They had many wonderful presents. They received dolls, toy soldiers, and picture books.

But Marie's favorite gift was from her dear godfather, Dr. Drosselmeier. It was a wooden nutcracker carved to look like an old soldier. What Marie did not know was that the nutcracker was enchanted!

That same evening there was a great Christmas party for Fritz, Marie, and their young cousins and friends. Everyone was having a great time.

Dr. Drosselmeier set up a stage and gave a wonderful puppet show. The little puppets danced while the children watched and laughed and clapped. Through the whole puppet show, Marie held her favorite gift, the nutcracker.

After the show Fritz started to dance around like a puppet. He took the nutcracker from Marie and held it high above her head. But then Fritz stumbled and dropped the nutcracker.

When Marie ran to pick up her favorite gift, she saw that its wooden jaw was broken. "Oh, no!" she cried. "Let me fix you, my poor nutcracker." She carefully tied the nutcracker back together with her handkerchief and put it under the Christmas tree.

Late that night Marie tiptoed down the stairs to the parlor. She picked up her nutcracker and saw that its jaw was not broken anymore!

The nutcracker also seemed to be changing. Before Marie's very eyes, the nutcracker became a handsome prince. He bowed to Marie and thanked her. He said that her kind act had broken a spell that had been cast over him.

Just then Marie saw an army of huge mice enter the room. They were led by a Mouse King, who had seven heads and carried a sword. The prince leaped forward to protect Marie.

Suddenly out of Fritz's gift box sprang a whole troop of toy soldiers that grew to life-size as soon as they stepped out of their box. The prince led the toy soldiers into a great battle against the Mouse King and his army.

And what a battle it was! Back and forth the two armies went.

Suddenly Marie saw her chance to help the prince. She took off her slipper and threw it with all her might at the Mouse King. Down he went! As quickly as they had come, the gray mice ran away.

The prince was now free to go home to his own land. "Would you like to come with me?" he asked Marie. "Oh, yes!" she said.

The prince raised his arms, and suddenly Marie found herself in the nutcracker prince's kingdom.

"Welcome to the Land of Sweets," said the prince. Marie saw sights she had never dreamed of. All the houses were made of peppermint sticks and chocolate.

Marie and the prince traveled down a river of lemonade in a little boat shaped like a seashell.

Finally they arrived at the sugar castle of the Sugarplum Fairy.

The prince told her how Marie had rescued him.

When the Sugarplum Fairy heard this, she decided to throw a big party. Everyone in the Land of Sweets came! The Sugarplum Fairy did a graceful fairy dance. Next came a parade of dancers from all over the world.

Marie had never seen such sights! There were chocolate dancers, candy dancers, and even enchanted dancing flowers.

Everyone joined in the dancing, but Marie was a little afraid to dance. Then the nutcracker prince came to her and said, "All this dancing is for you, Marie. You must dance, too."

So Marie and the prince whirled and whirled and whirled. . . .

. . . Suddenly Marie became quite dizzy and could no longer tell where she was. She rubbed her eyes, sat up, and found she was in her own parlor! And beside her was her nutcracker. Oh, could it all have been a dream?